I0617899

Sweet Slices of Life

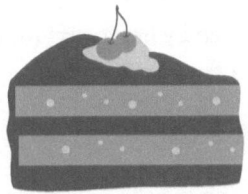

A COLLECTION OF REFLECTIONS, MUSINGS,
THOUGHTS AND POETIC INSPIRATIONS

OLUSOLA SOPHIA ANYANWU

ISBN: 978-1-915398-41-3

www.olusolasophiaanyanwuauthor.com

Contents

1. The New Year   1

2. Mary @ Full Term   3

3. Pray   4

4. Black Woman   6

5. Talking To Papa   8

6. Now I Am Yours   9

7. Smiling   11

8. My Father Is Different!   13

9. Olanna   15

10. Ivana   17

11. Ariella   19

12. in And Out Of Space   21

13. Festival   23

14. The Cross (For Good Friday)   24

15. You Are Elusive!   26

16. A Husband's Praise   28

17. New Times   31

18. December   33

19. Winter Eve   35

20. My Pleasure   36

21. But For You   37

22. Mystery   38

23. Black Skin   39

24. Out With The Girls!   41

25. Take A Walk With Me   43

26. Kelechi, My Seventh Grand   45

27. Eberechi, My Second Grand!   47

28. Olanna, My First Grand   48

29. Gym faith   49

30. A Song of Renewal   50

31. Another Son Dead   52

32. The Creeper   54

33. Limericks From Sophia   56

34. Race   58

35. Before The Beginning!   59

36. Flame   60

37. Asher   62

38. Oneme   64

39. Doyin   66

40. Martha   68

41. Isabella   70

42. Gabrielle   71

About The Poet   73

Other books by Olusola Sophia Anyanwu   75

Poetry   76

Dedicated to my entire family

With gratitude to the Holy Spirit for my inspiration

have a choice. You will dig, you will no longer go to the surface, and you will no longer bring your lies to the lounge and attempt to poison the minds of our people with impossible ideas. Understood?"

"Sure, I'll avoid the lounge. But I won't dig, and I *will* go to the surface."

He shook his head. "No. You don't understand, young lady. You will do as I say, or you will not live here anymore. I've talked with the others, Cece. We took a vote, and majority rules. You, my dear, are on probation. You *will* do as I say, or it has been agreed upon that you will be removed from the Sanctuary. Your whims are not worth the lives of the hundreds who live here and the thousands whose souls we keep safe. You have two days to fill a shift—either cleaning the air filters, harvesting hydroponics, or digging at the wall—or you're gone. It's that simple. We have rules here; and you follow those rules, or you're on your own—on the surface."

1. THE NEW YEAR

Receives the baton
Begins the 365 days marathon
At the starter's gun
On its predecessor's tracks
To the set clock of time
Like a new born
Ushered with joy

Scaling childhood hurdles
Covering teenage rounds
Shedding off adolescence layers
In summer heat and downpours
As a river flowing smoothly
Without diversion into
The embers of maturity

It finishes
Its last laps
Stirring the
World's excitement
Ending its cyclical race
Proffering the baton
To the receiver…

2. MARY @ FULL TERM

My time is near,
I hear my mind sigh.
Where is Angel Gabriel?
No dreams sent to Joseph,
No angel visits to me,
To say, 'It's well O maiden'.
Travelling soon to Jerusalem,
On Milly our donkey, but
No carriage sent,
No directions sent,
Who will do the birth delivery?
What clothing will God's son wear?
I have nothing except
This hand woven blanket
Knit by my hands…

3. PRAY

I pray because:
I am thankful
I am grateful
God is faithful
though am a sinner
God will answer
I have no other
divine helper
I need help
I need to pray
It is the way
to get to God
to pray
Prayer is obedience
to His Word
Prayer is relationship with God

Praying is talking to God
Draws me closer to God
Prayer acknowledges love
God is love
I know to get God's attention
I get God's protection
and His divine intervention
I affirm His goodness
When I get a miracle
God is awesome
He is pleased with me
God is loving
I pray to ask for His blessing
He is my Creator
I pray to ask for favour
I need His favour
I sometimes feel insecure
I pray because
God cares and listens
I pray to ask for His mercy:
to feel encouraged,
to receive power in His name,
and to enjoy being
under His authority!

4. BLACK WOMAN

The Black Woman
hails from black races -
the African, American and Caribbean.
Her footstool, the earth. She
rides on time's wings,
arising with the sun, and
ending with the moon.
Her sweat from labour is victory.
Her womb, the bearer
and carrier of her future.
Chilli spices her cooking
as hot as her love for family.
Her energy is legend
and her voice heard
in all corners of the earth.
Her heart larger than elephant ears
embracing all, as a river
embraces its shores,

with hugs and kisses.
She multitasks her hands
to produce, nurture and love,
merging talent and beauty.
She is sensually endowed.
She boldly embraces technology
education and ideology,
in her path to the sky.
The centre of the universe
is her home where
she spins unity and strength.
Her eyes speak volumes
more than words can vie for.
Her body language,
a comb of several tongues,
for each family member.
Deeper than the depths
of the earth is
her passion for family.
She is black in shades and hues
of light black to dark black.
Her teeth glimmer in her smiles.
They warm the heart of the beholder.
She is beautiful!

5. Talking To Papa

Papa God,
I ask for Your Peace.
and the grace to survive
this torment of waiting.
Help us Papa, to endure
the agony of expectation
and the temptation to give up.
Abba, please help us
not to forget that
You are the Prince of Peace.
You have a plan for our lives.
We can't control what
life throws at us, Papa.
Help us control what we can't.
Papa, we trust You, having no other choice.
We rely on Your timing.
Your timing is always right.

6. Now I Am Yours

My flesh doomed
My body corrupted
I was in darkness
Filthy and stinking
Of sins unimaginable
Doubt, unbelief, betrayal
And disobedience
You bound me in death chains
And slayed me
Your only son
As a lamb
Slain with the edge
Of the sharp steel
My blood crying out -
Your will is done, Papa
Turn Your face and see
Open Your ears and hear
Empty your heart of loath

Stretch Your arms to embrace
All Your creation
No more entwined in death's grip
To mock Your divinity
To steal your sovereignty
To shatter Your salvation dream
For Your beloveds

Now they see You, through me
They hear You
They feel You
They sense You
They are clean, through me
Their spirit is free
Dwelling in Your light
Now they share
Your eternal glory
Accept their gratitude
Accept their new faith,
Their devotion and sincerity
Forever more

7. SMILING

God is smiling at me
His smile radiates
Through the 11 o' clock sun
His smile is so infectious
It warms up my face
My whole body is ignited
With the warmth of His smile

The world is so bright
My mood is alright
With the sun's light
I smile back forgetting
February breathing
And blazing its cold breath
across me but I am smiling
at Papa God.

Abraham –God's friend
You came to me
More than in a million dreams
More than your creation of stars
in shadows, scenes and sights
calling, beckoning, teasing
even testing but I know
You are real
Your voice drew me out of doubt
Your smile armoured my spirit
Your words enriched my soul
Your friendship is everlasting
Your daring command
Strangely strengthens my spirit
I left all, but Lot , yet
You separated Lot from me
You want me for Yourself
Just me - YOUR Friend!

8. My Father Is Different!

I awoke this morning with
the desire to talk with
Father. He contacts me
in spirit at any time
unlike other fathers.
So unlike His other children,
I talk to Him differently.
He says He loves me.
Why have guilt about
speaking with Him differently?
He's not complaining, won't ever
because He too is different
from other parents!
He has the most offspring
and is omnipresent by spirit.
He's immanent, omniscient by spirit
and invisible to human sight.

I communicate at my leisure
and usually on my bed,
in the quiet of my spirit.
Dawn's not shed with light
yet. That's perfect for me.
Together, we run my affairs
through a common screen with
our minds walking together,
bringing in the best for me.
I remind Him about my
heart's desires, yearnings, fears
and my bold and daring requests.
He says He's different.
With Him, nothing is impossible.
Papa! Prove Yourself with proof
and give me my requests
in miracles beyond my imaginations.
You are my Almighty Father!

9. OLANNA

She is first born,
first daughter,
our first grand
and she starts a
new family and a
new generation.

Like the moon moving
round the earth and
the earth orbiting the
sun, she travels from
Dubai to UK and
from UK to Dubai.
Very tall, nimble and
graceful is she
as a gazelle.

A guru product of
Artificial Intelligence,
a proud combination of
two major Nigerian
breeds: Ibo and Yoruba.
A sapling rapidly
blooming. I see the
years flying. A woman
beautiful, confident emerges
as a butterfly from its
cocoon to reach the sky!

10. IVANA

She arrives as a balm
A melody to her parents
Filling the void
With her love and flinging out
The pain from hurting souls
Her birth is a blessing
An answered prayer

A heart's yearning and wish
Her star is luminously bright
In its wake, she brings joy
And contentment and laughter

Eneowaji, her mother crowns her
A skilled and talented artist
She is ,Adeoluwami,
the crown and glory of God

A beautiful princess endowed
With breath-taking hair, ballet limbs
camera eyes, a witty mind
That drips of wisdom
Born and bred in God's garden
She will be like the cedar of Lebanon
A pillar and light in her generation

11. ARIELLA

A child that mystifies adults
She is ahead of her age
Walks before she crawls
Reads before she talks
Writes before she's taught

Her brain, a magnet clutching
Absorbing, attracting
Everything and anything
Like a dry thirsty sponge
An artist that creates worlds
Outside and within her world

There she floats with the clouds
And smiles with unseen creations
Of pictures, numbers, music and art
A genius developing in strength
In a new generation to be explored

In a future Eden she will create
As a blessing to humanity
As she unravels the mystery of
God's light in dark minds.

12. IN AND OUT OF SPACE

The morning lies in bed awake
mating hotly with
my wayward thoughts
as it transports them through
mind space to Nigeria. Lingering. Sad.
Strolls back to London. The noise of their mindless
ramblings, loud in my ears
keep me restless: the next 96 hours?

My new baby is to be launched
to celebrate Black History Month. My thoughts
drag in the meal menu:
Chinchin, Puffpuff, Plantain Crips. And
Jollof? No. Just the finger ones. Pity.
I return to the moment in bed
with the morning.

It awoke long before me.
Its caresses warmed and turned my mind on.
My ears listen to the dawn -
Time is not deciphered. I won't peep.
Dawn is deep dark. I talk to God coz
I know He's awake too.
He too messes my mind.
He grabs the morning's fingers off my mind!
I submit to His coercing attention –
It brings pain. A helpless one
where I see my mind birthing thoughts
on Israel, Palestine, Ukraine, Russia and
other cities, countries, continents
all in needless havoc and hatred;
all in fear and dismay. My mind
questions God, seeking, probing
His presence in all these cauldrons
of hateful stews spewing out blood
of the innocent and the guilty.

It's not a nice place to dwell! Oh the mind power
that can shift, screen, sift, or slide over to the Artist
and create victory, peace, love, unity,
in rainbow colours -
where no evil can infiltrate life.

13. FESTIVAL

Thamesmead annual
festival
summer carnival
ignites its arrival
like a nocturnal
hibernating animal

Serves assorted delicacies- traditional
in talents, cultural
and multicultural
displays in natural
settings of musical
literary, drama and poetical
delights of a summer festival

14. The Cross (For Good Friday)

inspired from Pastor A. Bacon's sermon

What would have been our future?
At the cross we are all united by sin
All unified by our burdens of guilt
At the cross, Jesus took the crucifixion
Unburdened our sin
Refilled us with himself

We know who we are in him
We know what He's exchanged:
His strength for our weakness
His name for our name
His life for our death

His peace for our pain
His eternity for our immortality
His mercy for our destruction
His freedom for our slavery

To become new creatures
Eternal gratitude for the cross
We eat bread as His body
We drink wine as His blood
We live through this memory
Of the new covenant of the cross

15. You Are Elusive!

You are elusive
You come to me
Beckoning but I can't grasp you
You leave your slippery tail
Within my reach yet
Your head is out of my reach and
comprehension
I see you fully in my unconscious vapour state
But in solid state
You remain vaporised
Leaving the sketches of your body parts
In a missing jigsaw
Why do you steal my memory of you?
What use is a picture with no head and middle?
Even your tail eventually slithers out of my grip
Like leaking water dripping
I yearn for the whole of you

There lies the mystery of the unknown
There lies the secret of my maker concerning me
There lies the answer to my present and future
Joseph got it all right, why not me?
Give it all to me too!
The future making more sense
My footsteps are ordered aright
My mind is freed of deciphering the elusive

16. A Husband's Praise

Emmanuel Chima, Anyanwu
Son of Papa God
Anyanwu is sunshine
An extraordinary man
God's own name – Emmanuel
God with us
Name of worth
Once a church knight,
now God's Knight
Two deacon caps on head
Green shirt on trouser
Tuesdays and Thursdays
Suit and tie on Sundays
Shinny polished shoes always
Flew to UK 1987 Summer
Flew to UK 2004 Spring
To build a home
Caring, faithful and loyal husband

To his Obidia: Olusola Sophia

Writer, poet and life partner

Captured at the garden of Unife

Hooked her with his ring in 1983

Son of Madam Philomina

And Sir Patrick

From his loins birthed five

A loving father to:

Father to Francis

Father to Augustus

Father to Stephen

Father to Sharon

Father to Philomina

A very doting Grandpa

Olanna in 2014

Eberechi and Chima in 2016

Chioma in 2017

Chinwe and Chinomso in 2019

Kelechi in 2021:

Olanna, Eberechi, Chima

and more coming

His barn is full and his cup overflows

A handsome man

Infectious laugher always

President Chief Commander of

E.C Anyanwu Clan
Proud driver of Ford Mondeo,
2 chassis Vauxhall Astra cars
A formidable educationist
An expert DIY
Son of Okrika Nweke's soil
Member Akpim UK
Member Emmanuel Baptist Church
Thamesmead, London
Born and bred in Nigeria
Educated in Western Nigeria
A saint with a heart for God
Diligent in his dedication
In seeking the kingdom
Knees on prayers
Day and night interceding
For nations and all humanity
For family and friends
A noble man
Very dear and precious
To the church of Christ community
To his wife, children, in laws and grands
He is the apple of God's eye
His anointed servant
A honourable son of Papa God

17. NEW TIMES

The winds of season change
are the bells ringing the age
for a new chapter's birth.
for a new dawn on earth.

It blows new sincerity
of purpose and integrity.
New hopes arise
like the sun's rise
to begin a new day.

It spreads its rays
of affection,
ushering new reflections,
and dispelling old ways
and lingering doubts.

The winds of change
emerging from the South,
East, West and North
come calling forth
and equipping all to grip
the challenges of New Times.

18. December

In the boat with so many
Too many to count
All starting this journey
To get across to the shore
To a new tomorrow
Of a pregnant dawn that
Will birth many tomorrows

Who'll cross over?
Who'll be left behind?
December is greying by the day
To join its predecessors forever
Where history lives
Where memory breathes
Where the present
Joins the forgotten past
It's everyone's prayer
To be carried safely

On December's waves

As December plucks out
The boat gets lighter
Passengers fewer
Duty is duty
December hearkens
To the voices of Destiny,
Divinity, Death and December dies
We journey to a new era of life

19. Winter Eve

Screeching and screaming, it ran
Wildly, unleashing its terrifying howls
On human ears. Its vehemence
Lashed on trees, buildings, people and
Anything in its paths. A force of
Extreme rage? Excitement? Or indiscipline?
Feet hurry and hasten
as havoc is created at its delinquency.
Nothing can still its violent temper
Running riotous everywhere
At the same time.
Only One has the command,
The power and authority over
The elements. Just two words
Spoken silently stills the loud uproar,
Gathers all the fury into a teacup.
The words 'Be Still' calms soothingly
Like cold milk on hot tea.

20. My Pleasure

When I ponder in wonder
Of the goodness and awesome
Power of the Holy Spirit
I am completely struck
Speechless but my soul
Arises to the Heavens in
Praise and pleasure
Glory and gratitude
For the talents
You deposited in me
That have birthed
Thousands of words
In books and booklets
For blessing these eyes
With grace to delight in
Multiple scores of reviews

21. But For You

Thank You Lord
for loving us!
Sometimes
You make us laugh!
Other times
You make us cry!
You give us joy but
You also allow us sorrow!
You make us strong when weak
You make us weak when strong
You dispel our frailties and doubts
Carrying us during
Terrifying waves and
Fierce raging storms of life
But for you…

22. Mystery

Where have you hailed from?
Your sudden appearance
Catches me unawares
Dazzling my sight
With your rays of beauty.
I drift in dazed awe
In your seven colourful seas
Rowing my euphoric senses
In the crest of your waves.
As I lie in your bow shaped arch,
I forget the mystery of
Your unknown origin and
The mystery of the rain
That heralds the imminence
Of your royal presence.
In you lies the oath and
Symbol for eternal peace
Between mankind and his maker!

23. BLACK SKIN

The black skin
draws the beholder's eyes in:
as to feast on its satin
drink in its cup of richness
swim in its myriads of wealth
dress in its silk and velvety robes
admire its glistening sheen
under the toil of its labour.

They desire its scent of victory
in manifold walks of life.
It sings its excellence globally
as it spills its unique success
in art, music, sport and culture.
Black skin like magnetic strings
pulls the beholder's feelings -
an experience of awesomeness.

A status symbol of beauty
surpassing the peacock's
coat of many bewitching colours
surpassing the highest dizziest heights.
It creates tantalising imaginations.
It invokes inspiring dreams.
It casts spells like a chameleon
during its changing seasons
In life's perilous journey,
between turbulence and calm.

From its scenes of youth
to its scenes of maturity,
it travels its platinum ages
and revered years ahead
with grace and strength.
The black skin
proud of it!

24. Out With The Girls!

Three of us
span two generations with time and age,
flow with blood from the east and west -
a mixture of culture clashes
from two worlds immersed in two
continents: Africa and Europe.

Three of us
women of faith with differing attitudes,
different perspectives but one heart beating for God.
Set out for the first time
to dine together, to chat and bond
like never before

Three of us
on a summer sunny Saturday June 17th 2023,
walk to Abbey Café, Abbey Wood.
What's each one thinking?

One at 65, 28 and 26. We bridge the gap
distanced by an alien culture.

Three of us
old fashioned ideologies, modern perspectives
shocking fashions fight modesty and personalities.
The shared meal of two coffees, one chocolate,
one brekky brunch, one pancake brekky,
one trad brekky is a love feast.

Three of us
oblivious of time chat and churn
laughter out of full bellies. Get the wiser of each one
as we dive deep into our soul's depths
uncovering and shedding off the layers
that make us as strangers.

Three of us proffer hope with a cord woven tightly
with love.

25. Take A Walk With Me

Dawn awakes the birds –
magpies, crows, pigeons, blackbirds...
They wake the neighbourhood with
their cries, coos, chirps, calls.
I watch them gossip,
chat, chase and challenge
each other in their world.

Above, the still sonorous drones
of planes visible and invisible,
compliment their devotions.
Soon the vicinity wakes
drowning the atmosphere
with metallic sounds
from four and two wheels.
Houses now stir
with urgent voices
readying for work or school -

the occasional brawling
of an unwilling child.
The train tracks its way
reminding neighbours
their time of stirring.
The sky is summer
white and blue.

The greens are
awaiting their own
rustling to stir.
Soon, school feet and school runs
will begin to rave to their destinations.
As for me, while I have breath,
I'm grateful and thankful
for the privilege
to witness the awakening
of another dawn…

26. Kelechi, My Seventh Grand

A bone of my bone mischief wise
He is as fast as an hare
Never caught at his tortoise tricks
I feed him with delight as
He downloads in pleasure
Balls of swallow and melon soup
I slip into his small mouth
In quick successions

My love and warmth swell to the brim
He throws in a quick hat trick
At a chance of my averted eyes
My eyes open to find the mischief done
The cup empty, the soup bowl full
He earns a mere light tap

I see him in 2 decades at 21
He's not a fledgling
Coming out of babyhood
or emerging from childhood
He's a man!

27. Eberechi, My Second Grand!

Lovable and excitable
A bundle of life and energy
Like a puppy
Ever smiling to win your smile
Loves a cuddle and loves to give one
A princess with a mind older than her years
Her eagle eyes miss nothing
As they twinkle with mischief
Everything interests her except the dark
Easy to please and very caring
Easy to get along with and very playful
She's seven now and yet a child
She will fly with the years
And metamorphose to an adult
And become joined to her better half
To produce fruits after her own kind!

28. Olanna, My First Grand

My first of firsts
My first grand
Her coming elevated me
My status changed overnight
I became a grandmother
I saw her at 30 minutes old
Beautiful from birth
No birth wrinkles,
No scrunching and squishiness
9 years later a true princess
A blooming damsel with a soft heart
Pregnant with great promises
A 21st century hooker to technology
What will become you, two decades away?
Future and time can't tell me anything now
I pray to witness your own generation
Products from my first fruits

29. GYM FAITH

Keep believing for the best
Keep praying for dreams to happen
Keep encouraging yourself in the Lord
Keep speaking into your future
Keep standing in the gap
Love with all your heart
Keep trusting God with no doubts
Keep calling things that are not as if they are!

30. A Song of Renewal

[Inspired from Isaiah 40:31]

Wisdom, he stupidly shunned
His virgin tresses snipped
His divine strength sapped
His eyes stolen
He casts hope In the Lord, his God
Shatters a tower of enemies
In wisdom, he hoped in the Lord
He renewed his strength

Wisdom, she eagerly embraces
Strength escapes from waiting
Her flesh endlessly enticing
Her will refraining, engages her God
Saving a nation from its extermination
Its elimination from earth's surface
She emerges in history, a queen
Her faith soars on wings like eagles

In divine wisdom, hope and strength
A delivered nation ran from Egypt
An anointed shepherd ran from Saul
An adopted prince ran from Pharaoh
A widowed daughter in law ran from Moab
A devoted prophet ran from Ahab
A beloved son ran from wife of Potiphar
They ran but did not grow weary

Wisdom's call, wisely harkened
He walked the wilderness to Midian
Kingdom of Egypt left for shepherd's staff
Delivers a nation from eternal bondage
He walked the wilderness to Golgotha
Kingdom of Heaven left for shepherd's staff
Delivers a nation from eternal bondage
They walked but did not faint

31. Another Son Dead

His life at end
His loved ones crying
For the dying
Of their son in a hearse
The sorrow breaks their heart
What a waste to life

Caused by gang crime
All for the senseless reason
Of not belonging to the area
His coming to visit family in the area
Has cost this precious soul
A painful parting from earth

A deep loss and grief to loved ones
Nights and nights no sleep

There is a grief that can't be tamed
There is a vacuum that can't be filled
There's a cold heart that can't be warmed

There's a fear that won't go away
There are tears that can't be stopped
There's so much spilt blood in the land crying out
There are souls that can't rest in peace until
KNIFE AND GANG CRIME END!

32. THE CREEPER

Leaves its signatures
Everywhere it moves
Like a mourner's mourn
Signalling death's arrival
Like a cock's crows
Heralding dawn's arrival

Like the labouring womb
Foretelling a child's arrival
Or a dancing tree's boughs
Revealing its being tickled
By a crazed wind

The Creeper comes slowly, very slowly
Visible yet invisible
Riding on the year's back

Stamping marks on faces
Sprinkling spots and moles
Plucking out hair and teeth
Sprinkling grey and white

Ravaging and devouring
Deleting the signatures of youth
Dimming sight and hearing
Weakening will and mind
Encroaches suddenly
Creating bewilderment!

33. Limericks From Sophia

Ocean

Can this be a wonderful nightmare
My bed, a raft, floating me right here
The ocean in my room
Can't be swept with a broom
How can this much water be here!

Pot Belly

Pots of food don't bring this pot belly
It's the empty pot that is smelly
Not the belly button
It's the muddy monsoon
See and hear the truth from your telly

Thunder

We hear roars and murmurs of thunder
Sounds of crockery breaking asunder
Scramble swiftly upstairs
For it's not safe down there
Where the chairs are a few inches under

Mother Earth

She howls bellowing gallons of tears
Mother Earth shedding tons from her fears
Her kids play fire games
Her kids roll in gas games
They chase laughter and games with no ears

34. RACE

A seed planted in the ground of multiplication
sprouts and blossoms to an exotic tree of ambition.
Its fruits glitter and dazzle in the appreciations
of its beholders, in their exhortations.
Alas! A spot of sin breeds corruption.
Ambition plus Pride in their addition
degenerate towards a path of destruction.
Noah's family spared in the subtraction
to start the Saviour's generation for salvation.
The Creator turns this evil round to His satisfaction.
The Tower of Babel brings division and confusion,
from a myriad of languages with communication
in diverse tongues, birthing a population,
of manifold beings of every race in His creation!

35. Before The Beginning!

I found my imagination was a life cell floating in
the vast space and depth of Unknown.
I did not panic, as I darted at first aimlessly in the
middle of Nowhere.
A Word developed on me as I drifted in the Nothing.
Word was in me but outside me telling me:
Unknown, Nothing, Nowhere.
I looked inwardly and I had grown another cell. It
was my power!
No longer was I alone.
I was a threesome in one entity of my second cell.
I sat in front of my imagination to tweak the order
of Creation in my brain.

36. Flame

Fire flame flickers feeble as froth fizzling up in foam, timid in its dance as it sways unsteadily on its feet, like a new born lamb, licking its lips, nuzzling, awaiting the green sign.

Light of hope ladled out from its spring, lingering and reined by its rider, controlled by the strings propelling its force, heat and magnitude. It waits with open fluid palms.

Alighting unsteadily, haltingly, as if giddy from its dance, it's wary of a surprise blow. It accepts a token of love. Like a fuelled lamp, it bursts in a fiery flame igniting vision, warmth and passion.

Majestically like a king, it strides with strength, vigour, triumph and confidence, standing luminously bright, visible to every eye and lighting hearts with its peace and wisdom.

Emerging as Light illuminating, it ignites hearts with knowledge, understanding, dispels abhorring elements of evil and dispels darkness in its wake.

37. ASHER

My first grandson
His parent's first son
He's last born and only son
He's a hat joggler in his childhood
Between a First and a Last
Like a day shuttling between
Sunny and stormy spells
A lovable chap
A pup wanting to do as it pleases
A bold lion proud of its territory and roar
With cap of First
Asher spins marvel and awe
Don't ask for Last
A handsome prince is Asher
The waiting on
Confident assumption

Freedom of motion
Strutting cock amidst 12 hens
Spoilt for choice always
I'm amazed at his personality swings
Reeling to years ahead
Dangling to years below
The young grow
Shedding off old for new skins of maturity
Tomorrow
Asher is King
Tomorrow is Asher's dreams
Tomorrow, God willing
I will glory in the vision and reality
Of a billion prayers

38. ONEME

I appreciate Oneme
She is fond of my son
She's God's gift to me
For my first son, Ayodele
With perseverance and
With patience like the ant,
She builds her home with
Pampering and wisdom
She has come from afar
She who's her father's heart
Leaving all her jewels
Of family, land and self
Becoming one with her heart's throb, Emeka
With a mother's heart,
She pours out her devotion
Fending and tending endlessly
In faith, strength and courage

Ensuring God comes first
A fighter in her faith
On the wrong side as a porcupine
Her eyes are weighing scales
Judging motives and needs
Her hands multitask round the clock
Her true natural beauty and gentleness captivates
Like a general, she blows her breath
softly, quietly, calmly and assuredly
She embraces prudence,
Diligence and perseverance
She sacrifices pain for peace
A woman of good intentions
A bold woman who strips truth naked
A tough woman yet melts as butter
She is blessed with three beautiful talented priceless
gems
May you remain an emblem of light
Long life and prosperity with your Francis is your
portion
The joy of the Lord is always your strength
Keep the banner of love burning

39. Doyin

I adore Doyin
She her adores my son, Chima
Like her name, she is as honey
Sweet in her pleasantness and meekness
Wise in the knowledge of love and its art
An only child equal to ten sons
Any mother's delight and pride.
She blends her two cultures as one with wisdom
A discerning woman from youth
A daughter gifted to me by God
For our second son, Augustus
Blessed in house décor skills
Her hands multi task in assorted facets of life's
wonders
A daughter more than a daughter
A beauty in body and soul
She wears humility, patience and strength
She rides on the back of life with caution

She listens to my advice
She takes the Lord's counsel
She dishes discretion daintily
She adorns herself with the colours of 'wife material'
On the wrong side, darts appear
She is the pride of her Babe, Oluwatomisin
She is his Tomi's heartbeat
She runs her empire with precision
She spreads her tentacles of talent and wisdom
Cautiously and carefully along life's paths
She is a queen in her palace
Her hands are spiced in the art of culinary skills
She opens her doors with a golden heart
Her husband's desire is her pleasure
She is blessed with two beautiful talented priceless
gems
May your dreams and desires be fulfilled
May your days be long with your true love, Tomi
Keep the good going and glowing

40. Martha

I cherish Martha
She cherishes my son, Chidozie
She is a daughter
Ripe before her time
Plucked early from the childhood tree
As fearless as a lioness
She would hold her ground before
A troupe of elephants
A woman chosen by my God
For our youngest son, Stephen
Motherhood is natural to her
She brooks no leeway
And holds discipline with a firm hand
A hard worker in the home and office
She's a beauty in and out
She has no space for grudge and pretence
Her mind as crystal clear

Her words are bidding
On the wrong side
A pulsating boil
A daughter trustworthy
A daughter to be proud of
A daughter like an eagle
A daughter who'll hold the territory
A queen of her empire
A faithful worker in the Lord's vineyard
A woman with a loving heart
Olufemi's heart pulse
A mother to two beautiful, talented priceless gems
A true African beauty; a ringed neck
Holds confidently a proud head regally,
With cat slit eyes that see more than you can tell
A family lover, I'm proud of you
A quick learner and explorer of new depths
May God grant you your heart's desires, and
With long life with Nifemi, your true love
May your desires never be cut short
Keep the flag flying

41. Isabella

I beheld you on your day of birth
A bundle of amazing beauty
Arousing my delight and desire
To gaze gratefully forever at you –
God's miracle and mystery
I've watched you grow
As a tendered potted flower
Sprouting to seedling
I call you Chioma
You reflect God's beauty
In your smiles and surprisingly sweet ways
Greatly surpassing your years of seven
You are a wonder star
Blooming brighter every year
May your light perpetually shine
As you fulfil your destiny

42. GABRIELLE

She is our fifth grand
A treasure unfolding
Surprises of talent and promise
Her mesmerising smiles in
Pleasure and play are endearing
Her powerful voice is captivating
Commanding attention
A lover of cuddles and hugs
 She clutches the tail of babyhood
Yet she is a bold and daring
Invoking breath-taking gasps
What will she morph into?
This angel of beauty is blessed
A daughter of the Highest
She will soar like an eagle
Possess her inheritance
She will be a light in her generation

About The Poet

Olusola Sophia Anyanwu is an educationist, reviewer, encourager, bestselling author and poet. She loves reading books that grab her attention and interest. She says, "I love reading and writing stories that reflect the fascinating lives and relationships between people. Her writings also convey current issues in the world. She also writes Christian fiction and poetry to inspire hope and encouragement. The Holy Spirit of God inspires her. She is a member of the Association of Christian Writers [ACW], Society of Authors, National Poetry Library, Society of Poets, and TRELLIS Poetry Group, UK.

She has 20 books published. As a multi-genre author and poet, she writes on various assorted themes about life. Her works have been featured in the ACW eNews, ACW magazine, ACW blog, and the ACW Bookshop in the

UK and Amazon. Olusola Sophia says, "I want my readers to be carried to lofty heights in the realms of passion, love, faith, adventure, and laughter as they read each of my books. So get a dig in!"

She hopes her writing creates a positive influence on readers, enriches their lives, and gives encouragement and blessings. She is married and blessed with children and grandchildren. She is on Twitter, Facebook, LinkedIn, TikTok, YouTube, Goodreads, Amazon, and Instagram. More about Sophia and her books can be found on her website:

www.olusolasophiaanyanwuauthor.com

OTHER BOOKS BY
OLUSOLA SOPHIA ANYANWU

- Stories for Younger Generations
- Tales for Younger Generations
- Sophia's Fables for Younger Generations
- Stories for Older Generations
- Stories from the Heart
- The New Creatures
- We Can't Breathe
- Turning the Clock hands backwards
- The Confession
- The Crown
- Their Journey on Earth to Heaven
- The Robe
- Eliana's Redemption

POETRY

- Chameleon and Other Poems
- Sophia's Covid Poetry
- Poetry from the Heart
- Elegies and Dirges
- Echoes of Eco
- From the Womb
- Wings of Faith
- Poetry Matters